Dear Parents:

Congratulations! Your child is taking the first steps on an exciting journey. The destination? Independent reading!

STEP INTO READING® will help your child get there. The program offers five steps to reading success. Each step includes fun stories and colorful art or photographs. In addition to original fiction and books with favorite characters, there are Step into Reading Non-Fiction Readers, Phonics Readers and Boxed Sets, Sticker Readers, and Comic Readers—a complete literacy program with something to interest every child.

Learning to Read, Step by Step!

Ready to Read   Preschool–Kindergarten
• big type and easy words • rhyme and rhythm • picture clues
For children who know the alphabet and are eager to begin reading.

Reading with Help   Preschool–Grade 1
• basic vocabulary • short sentences • simple stories
For children who recognize familiar words and sound out new words with help.

Reading on Your Own   Grades 1–3
• engaging characters • easy-to-follow plots • popular topics
For children who are ready to read on their own.

Reading Paragraphs   Grades 2–3
• challenging vocabulary • short paragraphs • exciting stories
For newly independent readers who read simple sentences with confidence.

Ready for Chapters   Grades 2–4
• chapters • longer paragraphs • full-color art
For children who want to take the plunge into chapter books but still like colorful pictures.

STEP INTO READING® is designed to give every child a successful reading experience. The grade levels are only guides; children will progress through the steps at their own speed, developing confidence in their reading.

Remember, a lifetime love of reading starts with a single step!

Copyright © 2021 by Kristen Bell
Cover art and interior illustrations by Daniel Wiseman

All rights reserved. Published in the United States by Random House Children's Books,
a division of Penguin Random House LLC, New York.

Step into Reading, Random House, and the Random House colophon are registered trademarks
of Penguin Random House LLC.

Visit us on the Web!
StepIntoReading.com
rhcbooks.com

Educators and librarians, for a variety of teaching tools, visit us at RHTeachersLibrarians.com

Library of Congress Control Number: 2021940661
ISBN 978-0-593-43441-3 (trade) — ISBN 978-0-593-43442-0 (lib. bdg.) —
ISBN 978-0-593-43443-7 (ebook)

Printed in the United States of America
10 9 8 7 6 5 4 3 2 1

STEP INTO READING®

2 STEP

READING WITH HELP

The New Puppy

by Kristen Bell and Benjamin Hart

illustrated by Daniel Wiseman

Random House 🏠 New York

Penny and Mateo are
kind to animals.
That makes them
feel purple.

5

Today Mateo wants
to adopt a puppy!
He wants to be
a purple puppy brother.

What does a purple
puppy brother do?
He asks questions.

Does the puppy
like kids?
Yes!
Treats?
Yes!

Mateo chooses to
adopt the puppy.

The puppy is
excited to go
to a new home.

The purple puppy
has questions, too.

What time is supper?

Mateo loves to play
with his purple puppy.

The puppy loves
to make Mateo
and his friend Penny
laugh!

Mateo works hard
to take care of
his puppy.

Working hard
makes him
feel purple.

The puppy
works hard, too.
She helps Mateo
find a sock!

Sometimes Mateo needs
to speak up for his puppy.

She is a little shy.
No pats today.

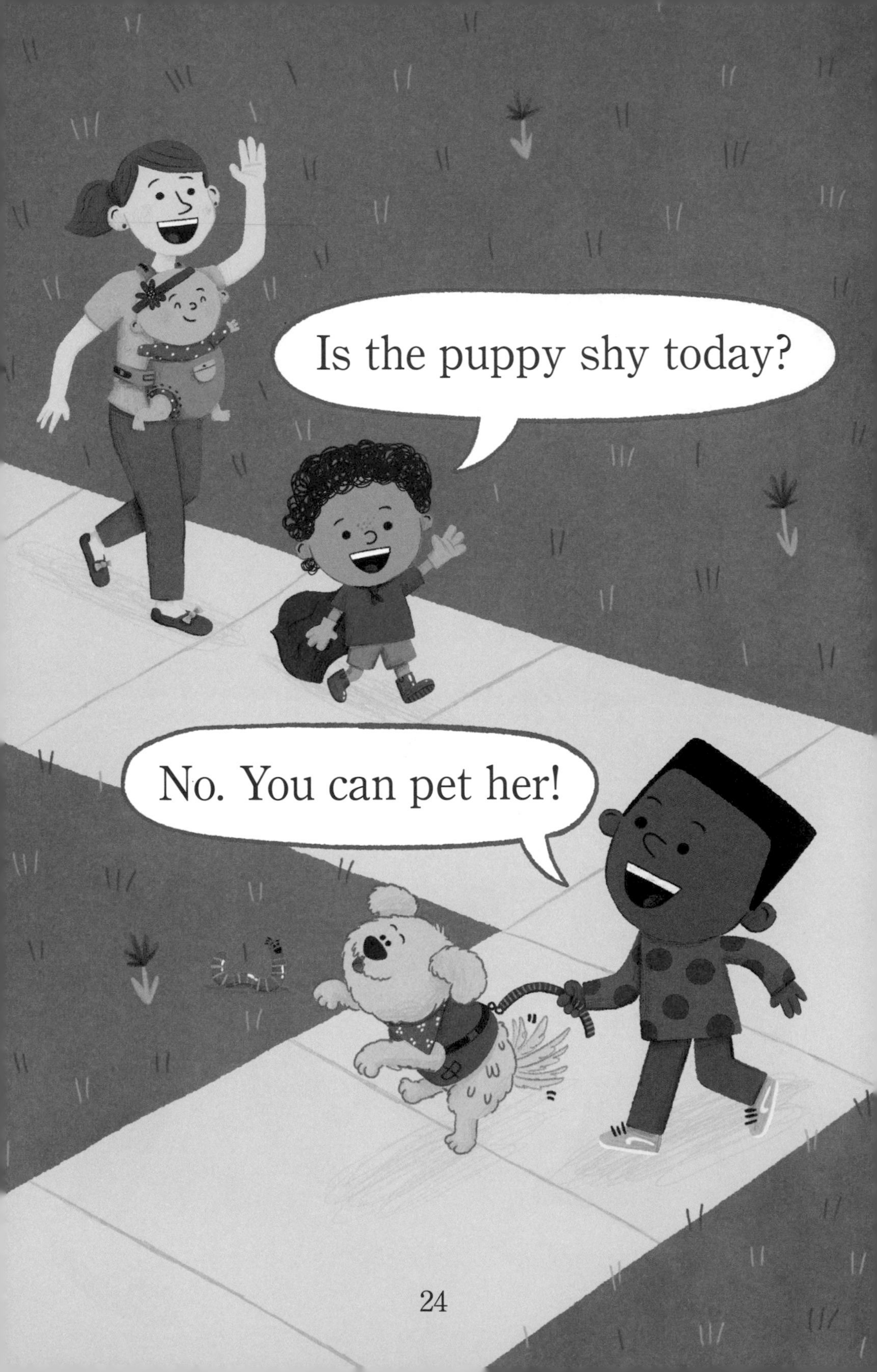
Is the puppy shy today?
No. You can pet her!

Sometimes Mateo's puppy
speaks for herself!

Mateo can always
be himself
with his puppy.

Mateo knows
his puppy will always
be herself, too.

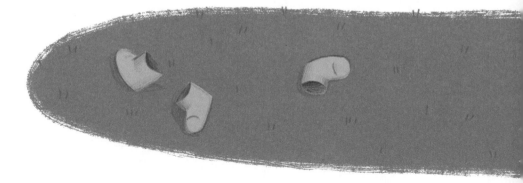

They both feel purple
when they are
themselves!

Purple puppies make
the best friends!

So do purple people!